Sleep-over Mouse

Written by Mary Packard
Illustrated by Kathy Wilburn

My First
READER

SCHOLASTIC INC.

New York Toronto London Auckland Sydney
Mexico City New Delhi Hong Kong Buenos Aires

ISBN 0-516-24499-X

Text copyright © 1994 by Nancy Hall, Inc.
Illustrations copyright © 1994 by Kathy Wilburn.
All rights reserved. Published by Scholastic Inc. SCHOLASTIC and associated
logos are trademarks and/or registered trademarks of Scholastic Inc.

12 11 10 9 8 7 6 5 4 3 2   3 4 5 6 7 8/0

Printed in the U.S.A.   61

First Scholastic printing, September 2003

Meet little Squeak.

He's a sleep-over mouse.

Squeak loves to sleep over

at anyone's house.

He loves to share toys.

He loves to share treats.

He loves to make noise.

He makes tents with sheets.

A sleepover is fun.

There is plenty to do!

Squeak loves to play.

He loves to sleep, too.

Can sleep-over mouse

sleep over with you?

ABOUT THE AUTHOR

Mary Packard has been writing children's books for as long as she can remember. Packard lives in Northport, New York, with her family. Besides writing, she loves music, theater, animals, and, of course, children of all ages.

ABOUT THE ILLUSTRATOR

Kathy Wilburn grew up in Kansas City, Missouri, where she began her artistic career with Hallmark Cards after graduating from the Rhode Island School of Design. She currently lives in Portland, Oregon, where she works as a children's book illustrator.